PATTY PANDA GETS A POTTY!
熊貓派蒂的新便盆!

WRITTEN BY VICKY WU
吳詩婷　文

Distribution by KDP Amazon and Ingram Spark – P.O.D.

Printed in the United States of America
Title: Patty Panda Gets A Potty
Author: Vicky W. DiDonato
Translator: Howard Chen and Evelyn Lu

Ebook ISBN: 978-1-7365756-1-1
Paperback ISBN: 978-1-7365756-0-4
Hardcover ISBN: 978-1-7365756-2-8

Publisher: Bilingual Bear Cat LLC

Book description: Patty Panda Gets a Potty: A rhyming story in Chinese and English about a girl who experiences the emotions of potty training for the first time.

This book is dedicated to Reagan Mei, my inspiration
and source of endless joy.

I am grateful to Uncle Howard and Aunt Evelyn for the
translation help, and to my parents for supporting my
dreams even though I never became a doctor.
V.W.D.

叮噹一聲鈴響了，
dīng dāng yì shēng líng xiǎng le

送來包裹一大個。
sòng lái bāo guǒ yí dà ge

Ding dong, doorbell! A package arrived.

何不把它拆開呢，看看裏面是甚麼？

Shall we unwrap it and see what's inside?

送你便盆作禮物，以後不再用尿布。

It's a potty for Patty, since diapers are done.

Big girls wear undies, it's so much more fun!

台灣小孩真能幹，很早就不包尿片。

Babies stop diapering early on in Taiwan.

阿ㄚˊ媽ㄇㄚ也ㄧㄝˇ說ㄕㄨㄛ有ㄧㄡˇ夠ㄍㄡˋ讚ㄗㄢˋ， 他ㄊㄚ們ㄇㄣ˙一ㄧ歲ㄙㄨㄟˋ開ㄎㄞ始ㄕˇ練ㄌㄧㄢˋ！

Grandma tells Mama
they start practice at one!

媽ㄇㄚ 咪ㄇㄧ 覺ㄐㄩㄝ 得ㄉㄜ 不ㄅㄨ 必ㄅㄧ 急ㄐㄧ，準ㄓㄨㄣ 備ㄅㄟ 好ㄏㄠ 了ㄌㄜ 再ㄗㄞ 練ㄌㄧㄢ 習ㄒㄧ。

mā mī jué de bú bì jí　zhǔn bèi hǎo le zài liàn xí

NO MORE DiAPERS

Potty Training 101

DDLER AND ME

Mama won't rush Patty before she's ready.

派蒂聰明又伶俐，
三歲以前沒問題。

By three she will get it, being smart and steady!

It's time to get started! There's no need to fear.

biàn pén fàng zài zhè lǐ la　　niào jìn lǐ miàn bié wài sā

便盆放在這裏啦，尿進裏面別外撒。

This is the potty, and your pee goes in here.

深深吸入一口氣，用盡身內吃奶力。

shēn shēn xī rù yì kǒu qì　yòng jìn shēn nèi chī nǎi lì

Mustering up all her might from within,

派蒂研究很仔細，以免掉到便盆裏。

Patty studies the potty to avoid falling in.

一邊蹲著一邊搖，屁股用力才有效。

Squatting and shaking, buns out in full force,

不再拖延不再耗，涓涓細流真奇妙。

without further delay, a stream forms a course.

派_{ㄆㄞ}蒂_{ㄉㄧ}嚇_{ㄒㄧㄚ}得_{ㄉㄜ}直_ㄓ發_{ㄈㄚ}毛_{ㄇㄠ}，一_ㄧ躍_{ㄩㄝ}而_ㄦ起_{ㄑㄧ}苦_{ㄎㄨ}哀_ㄞ嚎_{ㄏㄠ}。

pài dì xià de zhí fā máo　　yí yuè ér qǐ kǔ āi háo

The whole thing is scary,
so Patty leaps up and wails.

尿流滿地有如潮， 一攤攤又一條條。

niào liú mǎn dì yǒu rú cháo yì tān tān yòu yì tiáo tiáo

Pee is now everywhere,
forming puddles and trails.

chóu méi kǔ liǎn shuō bú yào, mā ma guì quàn xiān bié táo

愁眉苦臉說不要，媽媽跪勸先別逃。

Patty now frowns as Mama kneels down,

urging her please not to quit.

擦乾眼淚免煩惱， 回頭再試也很好。

cā gān yǎn lèi miǎn fán nǎo huí tóu zài shì yě hěn hǎo

"Don't worry dear,"
while drying her tears,
"try again later, in a bit."

情急之下舞亂跳，
qíng jí zhī xià wǔ luàn tiào

派蒂弄得一團糟。
pài dì nòng de yì tuán zāo

Patty's dance of distress made a huge mess,

媽媽建議小寶寶，稍事休息換一招。

mā ma jiàn yì xiǎo bǎo bao shāo shì xiū xí huàn yì zhāo

so Mama suggests getting some rest.

躲避疫情家裏蹲，媽咪復工用視訊。

When Mama returns
to a work call on Zoom,

一根金條衝鼻昏，摩卡異味滿室熏。

a tiny 💩 brown log appears to stink up the room.

chèn zhe dà jiā méi zhù yì   pài dì yì diǎn bù chí yí
趁著大家沒注意，派蒂一點不遲疑，

Before anyone sees,
without missing a beat,

趕快溜走為上計，霹啪霹啪不停蹄。

Patty scurries away, pit-pat go her feet.

tòng kǔ shēn yín yòng lì pái
痛苦呻吟用力排，

xiǎo liǎn fā hóng rú tián cài
小臉發紅如甜菜。

Grunting and
groaning,
face bright
as a beet,

yì jǔ dá biāo yǒu gòu shuài， dà gōng gào chéng xiào kāi huái！
一舉達標有夠帥， 大功告成笑開懷！

Patty succeeds,
achieving
the great feat!

xiǎo biàn dà biàn dōu gěi lì
小便大便都給力，

luò rù biàn pén méi wài yì
落入便盆沒外溢。

There's pee and there's poop,

but it's not on the floor.

媽媽開心給獎勵，
確認鉅細皆無遺。

mā ma kāi xīn gěi jiǎng lì
què rèn jù xì jiē wú yí

Mama offers a reward,
and confirms
there's no more.

Patty beams proudly, spirits lifted with hope.

xiàn zài xiān bǎ shǒu xǐ hǎo， qǐng nǐ gěi wǒ xiāng féi zào

現在先把手洗好，請你給我香肥皂！

Let's wash our hands now, please pass the soap!

VICKY WU DIDONATO is an American author based in
New York City. Born to immigrants from Taiwan, Vicky believed
it was important that her biracial children could understand their
grandparents' native language and culture. Not finding many
books that fit such criteria, she set out to write some herself. Her
writing aims to capture universal stories about childhood and
by extension, parenthood. Vicky's bilingual books are written
in English and traditional Chinese accompanied by zhuyin and
pinyin so that readers of all levels can learn together.

@pattypandabooks

CPSIA information can be obtained
at www.ICGtesting.com
Printed in the USA
LVHW070716061122
732476LV00004B/47